the
Aukipi
Dictionary

AN OFFICIAL AUK MODU LANGUAGE GUIDE

compiled by
e.j.bertch & m.e.hartz

earth=yuta

repetition to emphasize meaning?

plant symbology?

airy style indicative of 'vidara

fire=mura

bold and primitive

Introductory Remarks
Aukipi and the Tamariki of Lost Island

The Tamariki are such an elusive species, that it was a labor of love indeed to gather enough information to fill even a small booklet with Aukipi. Our first clumsy attempts at contact were woefully unsucessful. However, after learning the tradition of leaving offerings for these sneaky little guardians, our luck began to turn. The Tamariki, being extremely generous by nature, then quickly warmed to our presence, eager to share their language, culture, and island with us.

After five years and approximately 42,000 hours, we are only just beginning to understand Aukipi. It is an expressive, whimsical language which consists of words, heiroglyphs, and runic symbols. For the most part pronunciation is phonetic, with the addition of some gutteral sounds made deep in the throat.

We have compiled herein a comprehensive vocabulary, suitable for the average Auk Modu guest who wishes to try their hand –or tongue– at the local language. This is by no means a complete record of Aukipi. After all, one can hardly expect to learn an ancient language in just a few short years.

It is worth noting that Aukipi has been adopted by the Udara, the Awa, the Yuta, and the Mura people as well. Once you master the dialect you will be able to sucessfully communicate with the inhabitants of all 5 realms in their own tongue.

Marikawa ke ukau! [adventure awaits]
– M.E. Hartz & E.J. Bertch

Aukipi to English

translated alphabetically

A

a (ah) {artcl}: the

abok (ah-BAWK) {v}: to anger

ade (ah-DEH) {v}: to help

agi (ah-GEE) {v}: to begin

ago (ah-GOH) {v}: to end

aga (ah-GAH) {adv}: although

agula (ah-GOO-lah) {n}: eagle

ahio (ah-HEE-oh) {adj}: old

ai (ah-EE) {prep}: in

a'i (AH-ee) {prep}: on

akili (ah-KEE-lee) {v}: to like or enjoy

akilimu (ah-KEE-lee-moo) {adj}: favorite; best liked

amara (ah-MAR-ah) {n}: flying machine; specific to Udara realm

amata (ah-MAH-tah) {adj}: nice; pleasant

ana (ah-NAH) {n}: love

anapi (ah-NAH-pee) {v}: to love

ara (AH-rah) {v}: to open

aria (ah-REE-ah) {n}: a flower

aroki (ah-ROH-kee) {n}: nomad; specific to the Awa realm

arotu (ah-ROW-too) {n}: explorer

ata (AH-tah) {v}: happy

ata'awi (AH-ta'AH-wee) {n}: congratulations

atana'hi (ah-tahNAH'hee) {n}: harmony; balance

auk (awk) {v}: lost

auro (AH-roh) {n}: ear

auroto (ah-ROH-toh) {v}: to listen

awa (AH-wah) {n}: water

awaati (ah-WAH-tee) {n}: otter

awalla (ah-WAH-la) {n}: ship

awi (AH-wee) {n}: day

awi'zuz (ah-WEE-zooz) {n}: celebration

azuli (ah-ZOO-lee) {adj}: turquoise

Bakiti (bah-KEE-tee) {n}: Rainy Season or Water Blessings; measure of time; approx. 2.5 months of rain

balawi (bah-LAH-wee) {n}: night

balo (BAH-loh) {adj}: black

balomu (bah-LOH-moo) {adj}: dark

bama (BAH-mah) {n}: burger

banu (BAH-noo) {n}: species of tropical tree

banuza (bah-NOO-zah) {n}: type of insect

bawa (bah-WAH) {adv}: under or beneath

baza *(BAH-zah)* {n}: *brain*

bizo *(BEE-zoh)* {n}: *alcohol; most commonly beer*

bugroot *(BOO-groot)* {n}: *type of spice*

buzi *(boo-ZEE)* {n}: *horse*

da *(dah)* {adj}: *three*

damu *(DAH-moo)* {v}: *to ride upon*

damu *(dah-MOO)* {n}: *a ride or attraction*

di *(dee)* {adj}: *one*

didi *(DEE-dee* {adj}: *two*

dido *(DEE-doh)* {adj}: *four*

didu *(DEE-doo)* {adj}: *nine*

dipi *(DEE-pee)* {v}: *to drop; to dive, as into water*

do *(doh)* {adj}: *five*

doda *(DOH-dah)* {adj}: *eight*

dodi *(DOH-dee)* {adj}: *six*

dodidi *(doh-DEE-dee)* {adj}: *seven*

dol *(dohl)* {adj}: *sweet*

dolummi *(doh-LOO-mee)* {n}: *candy*

domiru *(doh-MEE-roo)* {v}: *to dream*

du *(doo)* {adj}: *ten*

e'ora *(eh'OH-rah)* {n}: *guild*

e *(eh)* {n}: *you*

e'e *(EH'eh)* {n}: *your*

eeki eeki *(EE-kee EE-kee)* {n}: *giant squid*

eekotomi *(EE-koh-TOH-mee)* {adj/adv}: *long; length; distance between two points*

ele *(EH-leh)* {v}: *fun*

en *(ehn)* {v}: *do*

eo *(EH-oh)* {conj}: *or*

etini *(eh-TEE-nee)* {n}: *children; kids*

eto *(EH-toh)* {n}: *people; referring to humanoids*

ezo *(EH-zoh)* {n}: *animal*

ezuz *(eh-ZOOZ)* {n}: *ourselves*

ga *(gah)* {conj}: *and*

gaba *(GAH-bah)* {v}: *hungry*

Galti *(GAHL-tee)* {n}: *Season of Abundance or Renewal; measure of time; approx. 2.5 months of growth*

gama *(GAH-mah)* {n}: *game*

gatana *(gah-TAH-nah)* {n}: *team*

gatora *(gah-TOH-rah)* {n}: *clan*

gobi *(GOH-bee)* {n}: *a small, bat-eared rodent*

golapa *(goh-LAH-pah)* {n}: *type of tree; identified by its helicopter seed pods*

ha *(hah)* {n}: *foot*

Haku

haku (HA-koo) {n}: hawk
hani (HAH-nee) {n}: toe
hewa (HEY-wah) {n}: cloud
hi (hee) {n}: hand
hini (HEE-nee) {n}: finger
hio (HEE-oh) {n}: wheel; circle
hul (hool) {adj}: cold
hulta (HOOL-tah) {adj}: fear
hummi (HOO-mee) {n}: clue
hutinka (hoo-TEEN-kah) {n}: keepers
hutora (hoo-TOH-rah) {n}: truth
hutu (HOO-too) {n}: word
hutuve (hoo-TOO-veh) {n}: verb
i (ee) {prep}: of
ikoo (EE-koho) {n}: magic
ilut (ee-LOOT) {v}: to shine
imi (EE-mee) {v}: to observe; to look
imitu (ee-MEE-too) {v}: to follow
ima (EE-mah) {n}: eye
imo (EE-moh) {v}: to see
in (een) {adj}: less
ingata (eeng-GAH-tah) {v}: to preserve; to save
ini (EE-nee) {adj}: little or small
ipi (EE-pee) {v}: to speak
kaga (KAH-gah) {n}: a type of drum; specific to the Mura realm

Kummaho

kal (kahl) {adj}: hot
kaluna (kah-LOO-nah) {n}: mermaid
kapa (KAH-pah) {n}: bat
kapulele (kah-poo-LAY-lay) {n}: butterfly
karo (KAH-roh) {adv}: why
ka'ro (kah'ROH) {adv}: why
ke (keh) {adv}: is; are; to be
ke'eto (keh'EH-toh) {n}: kingdom
ki (kee) {adv}: here
kin (keen) {n}: who
kinaro (kee-NAR-oh) {adv}: where
kino (KEE-noh) {adv}: what
kinop (kee-NAHP) {n}: a guide
kinto (KEEN-toh) {v}: to have; to possess
ko (koh) {adv}: how
koni (KOH-nee) {adv}: when
koporu (koh-POH-roo) {n}: body
kukui (koo-KOO-ee) {adj}: crazy
kukuo (koo-KOO-oh) {n}: type of small, sweet berry; usually pink in color
kuluma (koo-LOO-mah) {n}: music
kummaho (koo-MAH-hoh) {adj}: far or distant

Kuto

kuto (KOO-toh) {v}: to respect

laguna (lah-GOO-nah) {n}: a hidden pool; specifically in a forested area

lakoki (lah-KOH-kee) {n}: locker

laku (LAH-koo) {n}: hair

lami (LAH-mee) {adj}: better

lamia (lah-MEE-ah) {adj}: best

lamo (lah-MEE-oh) {adj}: good

lamo'toppu (lah-moh'TOH-poo) {v}: to achieve; an achievement

lamoragi (lah-moh-RAH-gee) {n}: paradise

laru (LAH-roo) {n}: color

larunahi (lah-roo-NAH-hee) {n}: a rainbow

lau (LAH-oo) {v}: to visit

Lazuli (lah-ZOO-lee) {n}: mystical water source of the Awa

le'emuli (leh'eh-MOO-lee) {n}: a line or queue

lili (LEE-lee) {n}: leg

lokolo (loh-KOH-loh) {n}: caterpillar

luho (LOO-hoh) {n}: palm tree

lumaragi (loo-mah-RAH-gee) {v}: enlightenment

Matu've

lumari (loo-MAH-ree) {v}: lucky; to be enchanted

lumo (LOO-moh) {v/adj}: to illuminate; light

lumodoz (LOO-moh-dohz) {n}: star

lumodoz pazaki (loo-MOH-dohz PAH-zah-KEE) {n}: starfish

luzio (LOO-zee-oh) {n}: a type of nut

mako (MAH-koh) {v}: to have courage; to be brave

makoki (mah-KOH-kee) {v}: to challenge

ma'kove (MAH-koh-veh) {v}: to fight

marikawa (mah-ree-KAH-wah) {n}: an adventure

maroki (mah-ROH-kee) {n}: monkey

marubu (mah-ROO-boo) {v}: thank you; thanks

mata (MAH-tah) {n}: mom; mother

matamu (mah-TAH-moo) {n}: grandmother

mati (MAH-tee) {n}: realm

matua (mah-TOO-ah) {n}: ground

matu've (mah-TOO-veh) {v}: to plant; to dig

Maz

maz (mahz) {adj}: more

me (meh) {v}: let; to allow

medidi (meh-DEE-dee) {n}: one season; measure of time; approx. 2.5 months

mi (mee) {n}: her/she

migaro (mee-GAH-roh) {n}: secret

minoo (MEE-noo) {n}: sister

mitu (MEE-too) {n}: hers

miwu'u (mee-WOO'oo) {n}: girl

modu (MOH-doo) {n}: island

mu (moo) {adj}: big or great

mu'la (MOO'lah) {adj}: many

mu'lamia (MOO'lah-MEE-ah) {adj}: ultimate

mupazu (MOO-pah-zoo) {n}: journey

mur (mer) {n}: sun

mura (MER-ah) {n}: fire; people of the fire realm

nahi (NAH-hee) {n}: all

nahi'awa (NAH-hee'AH-wah) {n}: sea; ocean

nahi'medi (NAH-hee'MEH-dee) {n}: a turn; measure of time; approx. one year

nala (NAH-lah) {adv}: please; a request

narin (nah-REEN) {n}: tradition

Okomu

ni (nee) {n}: no; a refusal

ni'ta (NEE'tah) {v}: to hate

ni'vin (NEE'veen) {adj}: countless

niva (NEE-vah) {n}: name

nubu (NOO-boo) {n}: number

nubuzi (noo-BOO-zee) {n}: sea horse

nui (NOO-wee) {adj}: well-known

nuna (NOO-nah) {n}: moon

Nuna (NOO-nah) {n}: Twilight Season; approx. 2.5 months without the sun

o (oh) {n}: me

oo (oo) {n}: my

oba (oh-BAH) {adj}: over

obaki (oh-BAH-kee) {adj}: there

oga (OH-gah) {adv}: before

ogaba (oh-GAH-bah) {adv}: after

ohu (OH-hoo) {n}: frog

okapa (oh-KAH-pah) {n}: jungle deer

oko (OH-koh) {adj}: bad

okomi (oh-KOH-mee) {adj}: worse

okomia (oh-KOH-mee-ah) {adj}: worst

okomu (oh-KOH-moo) {n}: evil

Aukipi -- English

okotoki (OH-koh-TOH-kee) {adj}: greed

okotopu (OH-koh-TOH-poo) {adj}: arrogance

oopu (OO-poo) {n}: friend

ora (OH-rah) {n}: gold

oragi (oh-RAH-gee) {adv/v}: life; to live

pa (pah) {adj}: red

pahi (PAH-hee) {v}: to smile

pala (PAH-lah) {n}: sand

papura (pah-PUH-rah) {adj}: purple

pata (PAH-tah) {n}: dad; father

patamu (pah-TAH-moo) {n}: grandfather

payaga (pah-YAH-gah) {adj}: orange

pazaki (PAH-zah-KEE) {n}: referring to all fish

pazu (pah-ZOO) {n}: path

petra (PEET-rah) {n}: a species of bird, usually small, vibrantly colored

pezaki (peh-ZAH-kee) {n}: a species of fish, usually fuchsia in color

pi (pee) {n}: he/him

pikopua (PEE-koh-POO-ah) {n}: hello; a greeting

pinoo (PEE-noo) {n}: brother

pitu (PEE-too) {n}: his

piwu'u (pee-WOO'oo) {n}: boy

poko (POH-koh) {n}: head

pokolu (poh-KOH-loo) {n}: mouth

pula (POO-lah) {n}: span; measure of distance; approx. 3 feet or the length of an arm

pulaga (poo-LAH-gah) {n}: tick; measure of distance; approx. 2 inches or the length of a thumb

ratana (rah-TAH-nah) {v}: to recycle

razo (RAH-zoh) {n}: arm

re'eto (reh'EH-toh) {adv}: again; once more

reroke'eto (reh-ROH-keh'EH-toh) {n}: civilization

retaro (reh-TAH-roh) {v}: to save

riri (REE-ree) {v}: to sing

ririve (ree-REE-veh) {v}: to dance

ro (roh) {adv}: yes; affirmative

rumpu (ROOM-poo) {n}: dolphin

ruzo (ROO-zoh) {n}: elbow

ta (tah) {n}: heart

ta'ana (TAH'ah-nah) {n}: family

taga'a (tah-GAH'ah) {n}: gods; higher beings

Aukipi — English

Tagipi

tagipi (tag-GEE-pee) {n}: motto or phrase

tago (TAH-goh) {n}: wisdom

tago uto (TAH-goh OO-toh) {n}: wise teacher; shaman

taguna (tah-GOO-nah) {n}: species of bird

tamariki (tah-mah-REE-kee) {n}: spirit; magical inhabitants of lost island

tamatua (tah-mah-TOO-ah) {n}: home

tana'hewa (tah-NAH'heh-wah) {n}: floating city

tanahio (tah-NAH-hee-oh) {n}: the world

ta've (TAH'veh) {phrase}: change of heart

tazaga (tah-ZAH-gah) {n}: a place

te (teh) {adv}: to

tempi (TEHM-pee) {n}: time

tempiagi (tehm-pee-AH-gee) {phrase}: an expression; the beginning of time

tempiago (tehm-pee-AH-GO) {phrase}: end of days

tempiko (tehm-PEE-koh) {adv}: forever; a long time

ti'ana (TEE'ah-nah) {n}: torso

Uda've

tikitam (TEE-kee-tahm) {v}: to play

titu (TEE-too) {n}: ticket

toki (TOH-kee) {n}: coin; money

tokini (toh-KEE-nee) {n}: change; an exchange of coin

tomi (TOH-mee) {adj}: short

topu (TOH-poo) {v}: to win

topu'u (toh-POO'oo) {n}: tower

topugo (toh-POO-goh) {n}: a temple; sacred building

topukuto (toh-poo-KOO-toh) {n}: an award

topukuto (toh-POO-koo-toh) {v}: to give award

toputi (toh-POO-tee) {n}: a winner

totara (toh-TAH-rah) {n}: a species of tree

totu (TOH-too) {n}: a species of bird; a toothed parrot

tuka (TOO-kah) {n}: a turtle

tuli (too-LEE) {n}: knee

tupi (TOO-pee) {v}: to bring

tuwit (TOO-weet) {n}: a type of spice

uda (OO-dah) {adj}: up

udara (oo-DAH-rah) {n}: air; people of the air realm

uda've (oo-DAH'veh) {v}: to climb

Udo'oz

udo'oz *(oo-DOH'ohz)* {n}: sky

udoz *(OO-dohz)* {v}: to fly; flying

ukau *(oo-KAH-oo)* {adj}: ready; prepared

ula *(OO-lah)* {adj}: strong

ummata *(oo-MAH-tah)* {v/n}: to drink; a drink

ummi ummi *(OO-mee OO-mee)* {n}: food

ummi'ke *(oo-MEE'keh)* {n}: a restaurant

ummi've *(oo-MEE'veh)* {v}: to cook; prepare food

ummiti *(oo-MEE-tee)* {v}: to eat; to feed

umo *(OO-moh)* {n}: a current; water or air moving in a direction; up-to-date

un *(oon)* {artcl}: a

unt *(oont)* {prep}: at

ura *(OO-rah)* {adj}: blue

ut *(oot)* {adj}: white

utoki *(oo-TOH-kee)* {v}: to know

utoko *(oo-TOH-koh)* {n}: knowledge

ut'pa *(OOT'pah)* {adj}: pink

va *(vah)* {conj}: for

vakat *(vah-KAHT)* {v}: to forge

ve *(veh)* {v}: to move; to walk

Weki'ni

vekulu *(veh-KOO-loo)* {n}: wild dog

veve *(VEH-veh)* {v}: to run

vewa *(VEH-wah)* {v}: to swim

veza *(VEH-zah)* {n}: snake

vin *(veen)* {adj}: zero

volago *(voh-LAH-goh)* {n}: a volcano

Voltariz *(vol-TAH-reez)* {n}: Sun Season; approx. 2.5 months of dry heat

wa'aki *(wah'AH-kee)* {adj}: weak

wabaku *(wah-BAH-koo)* {n}: a bad person; waste of space; a seat-filler

wahaari *(wah-HA-ree)* {n}: a greeting, welcome

wakapi *(wah-KAH-pee)* {n}: pride

wakatiki *(WAH-kah-TEE-kee)* {n}: restroom

waki *(WAH-kee)* {n}: a fool

waku *(WAH-koo)* {n}: a loser

walla *(WAH-lah)* {n}: a boat

wamopua *(wah-moh-POO-ah)* {n}: farewell; goodbye

wawago *(wah-WAH-go)* {v/n}: to die; death

wawat *(wah-WAHT)* {v}: to rest

weki'ni *(wah-KEE'nee)* {n/v}: an entry point; to enter

Weki'ut	Zuz

weki'ut (wah-KEE'oot) {n}/{v}: an exit point; to exit

wito (WEE-toh) {v}: to stop; to wait

wotoru'u (WEE-toh-ROO'oo) {adj}: slow

wub wab (WUHB-wahb) {n}: a blob fish

wuru (WOO-roo) {adv}: next

ya (yah) {adv}: yeah; sure; an agreement

yaga (YAH-gah) {adj}: yellow

yagura (yah-GUR-ah) {adj}: green

yanu (YAH-noo) {n}: feather

yik yik (YEEK yeek) {n}: a horned fox

Yom (yohm) {n}: Windy Season or Trade Winds; approx. 2.5 months of windy conditions

yuta (YOO-tah) {n}: earth; people of the earth realm

yuti (YOO-tee) {n}: forest; plants or foliage

yuti'ahio (YOO-tee'AH-hee-oh) {n}: the oldest part of the forest

yutini (yoo-TEE-nee) {n}: sapling; small or young tree

yutiwa (yoo-TEE-wah) {n}: seaweed

zaka (zah-KAH) {n}: a curse; an expression of frustration

zakar (zah-KAR) {v}: to be cursed; to curse someone

zakat'a (zah-kaht'AH) {n}: destruction

zavo (ZAH-voh) {n}: a shark

ziki (ZEE-kee) {n}: a type of spice

zu'ula (ZOO'oo-lah) {n}: strength

zuz (zooz) {adv}: together

zu'ula (ZOO'oo-lah) {n}: strength

zuz (zooz) {adv}: together

zakar (zah-KAR) {v}: to be cursed; to curse someone

zakat'a (zah-kaht'AH) {n}: destruction

zapi (ZAH-pee) {n}: pizza

zavo (ZAH-voh) {n}: shark

zelo (ZEH-low) {n}: french fries

ziki (ZEE-kee) {n}: a type of spice

zu'ula (ZOO'oo-lah) {n}: strength

zuz (zooz) {adv}: together

Quick Reference
phrases, words, lore & more

PRONUNCIATION GUIDE

Aukipi contains sounds and sentence structures similar to English, Spanish, and island languages such as Hawaiian and Samoan.

The Aukipi alphabet *does not* contain the letters:
C, F, J, Q, X, or S.

As such, "Ch" and "sh" sounds do not exist. Nor does "juh" as in "jam". An apostrophe between letters indicates a hiccup sound, as in "uh-oh".

The Aukipi accent is very musical, rhythmic, and expressive.

CONSONANT SOUNDS

Consonants are sounded out phonetically with these guidelines in mind:

'G' is always gutteral "guh".
'Z' acts as an 'S' but also as the English 'Z' as in "zipper".
'R' can be flat, as in English or rolled as in Spanish.

All other consonants follow basic English pronunciation sounds.

VOWEL SOUNDS

A = "AH"	I = "EE"
A'A = "AH-AH"	II = "EE"
AA = "AH"	
	O = "OH"
E = "EH"	OO = "OO"
E'E = "EH-EH"	
EE = "EE"	U = "OO"
	U'U = "OO-OO"

Pronunciation Notes:

THE LEGEND OF AUK MODU

Long ago a powerful evil threatened to destroy Lost Island (Auk Modu). The Tamariki, the island's magical, elusive guardians, sought help to defeat this evil from the 4 neighboring realms: the Udara Society, the Awa Navigators, the Yuta Merchants and the Mura Clan. Though the realms had been in conflict, they recognized the need for team work to defeat the evil monster, Volkanu, and save their home. With their combined elemental powers, they created the Ora Tika statue and managed to imprison Volkanu beneath the volcano.

The realms lived in peace for many years, but now the sacred statue has gone missing and the Island is in danger once again! This time, the Tamariki are counting on visiting guests to recover the Ora Tika idol and help save Auk Modu.

Kanu - unknown

rumors of banishment?

Tika - tamariki of stories

missing ...
the binding of ...

As their greed grew in strength, so too the evil lurking below

THE TAMARIKI & VOLKANU

Currently there are 22 known Tamariki, 20 of whom still exist today. Each Tamariki represents something best shared. Each realm has a specific Tamariki representative.

Details about Volkanu are scarce. It is known to be a destructive force, either composed of and/or able to manipulate molten lava.

"until it broke free"

USEFUL EXPRESSIONS

Where is ...?	*Kinaro ke ......?*
Where is the restroom?	*Kinaro ke a wakatiki?*
Where is the restaraunt?	*Kinaro ke a ummi'ke?*
Where is the gift shop?	*Kinaro ke a tingo'yupo?*
Where are the lockers?	*Kinaro ke a lakoki?*
Where is the picnic area?	*Kinaro ke a umi ke'etiki?*
Where are the children's rides?	*Kinaro ke a damu'i etini?*
Welcome to....!	*Wahaari te...!*
Welcome to Lost Island!	*Wahaari te Auk Modu!*
Welcome home!	*Wahaari ta!*
Welcome back!	*Wahaari re'eto!*
Welcome to my home.	*Wahaari te tamatua'oo.*
Welcome to the party!	*Wahaari te a awi'zuz!*
Adventure awaits!	*Marikawa ke ukau!*
Hello! My name is...	*Peekopua! O'o niva ke...*
Thank you.	*Marubu.*
My pleasure.	*O'o nala.*
May I help you?	*Ko ade'e?*
Respectfully,	*Kutomu,*
Happy Birthday!	*Ata'awiagi!*
I like you.	*O'akili e.*
Pleasure to meet you.	*Nala utoki e'e niva.*
Goodbye.	*Imo'e.*

THE BODY: A KOPORU

head	*poko* (POH-koh)	**hand**	*hi* (hee)
brain	*baza* (BAH-zah)	**finger**	*hini* (HEE-nee)
hair	*aku* (LAH-koo)	**torso**	*ti'ana* (TEE'ah-nah)
eye	*ima* (EE-mah)	**heart**	*ta* (tah)
ear	*auro* (AH-roh)	**knee**	*tuli* (TOO-lee)
mouth	*pokolu* (poh-KOO-loo)	**leg**	*lili* (LEE-lee)
arm	*razo* (RAH-zoh)	**foot**	*ha* (hah)
elbow	*ruzo* (ROO-zoh)	**toe**	*hani* (HA-nee)

COLORS: LARU

purple	*papura* (pah-POO-rah)	**white**	*ut* (OOt)
red	*pa* (pah)	**black**	*balo* (BAH-loh)
blue	*ura* (OO-rah)	**pink**	*ut'pa* (OOT'pah)
yellow	*yaga* (YAH-gah)	**turquoise**	*azuli* (ah-ZOO-lee)
green	*yagura* (yah-GOO-rah)	**gold**	*ora* (OH-rah)
orange	*payaga* (pah-YAH-gah)		

QUESTION WORDS: HUTU

who	*kin* (kEEN)	**where**	*kinaro* (KEE-nah-roh)
what	*kino* (KEE-no)	**why**	*karo* (KAH-roh)
when	*koni* (koh-NEE)	**how**	*ko* (koh)

QUICK REFERENCE

VERBS: HUTU VE

sing *riri* (REE-ree)
dance *ririve* (ree-REE-veh)
move/walk *ve* (veh)
run *veve* (VEH-veh)
dive/drop *dipi* (DEE-pee)
eat *ummiti* (DOH-dee)
fly *udoz* (OO-dohz)

look *imi* (EE-mee)
speak *ipi* (EE-pee)
swim *vewa* (VEH-wah)
ride *damu* (DAH-moo)
climb *uda've* (oo-DAH'veh)
dig *matu've* (mah-TOO'veh)

FOOD & DRINK: UMMI UMMI GA UMMATA

beer *bizo* (BEE-zoh)
water *awa* (AH-wah)
berry *kukuo* (koo-KOO-oh)
orange *payaga* (pah-YAH-gah)
spices *bugroot, tuwit, ziki*

candy *dolummi* (doh-LOO-mee)
burger *bama* (BAH-mah)
fries *zelo* (ZEH-low)
pizza *zapi* (ZAH-pee)

PLACES: TAZAGA

forest pool *Laguna* (lah-GOO-nah)
volcano *volago* (voh-LAH-go)
on the ocean *a'i un nahi'awa* (nah-HEE'AH-wa)
old forest *Yuti'ahio* (yoo-tee-AH'HEE-oh)
paradise *lamoragi* (lah-moh-RAH-gee)
island *modu* (MOH-doo)
forest *yuti* (YOO-tee)
realm *mati* (MAH-tee)
here *ki* (kee)
there *obaki* (MAH-tee)
home *tamatua* (tah-mah-TOO-ah)

PLANTS: YUTI

bush bali *(BAH-lee)*
flower aria *(AH-ree-ah)*
palm tree luho *(LOO-hoh)*
sapling yutini *(yoo-TEE-nee)*
tree (species) totara *(toh-TAH-rah)*
tree (species) banu *(BAH-noo)*
trees (general) golapa *(goh-LAH-pah)*
seaweed yutiwa *(yoo-TEE-wah)*

ANIMALS: EZO

sea horse nubuzi *(noo-BOO-zee)*
horse buzi *(boo-ZEE)*
butterfly kapulele *(kah-poo-LEH-leh)*
caterpillar lokolo *(loh-KOH-loh)*
giant squid eeki eeki *(EE-kee EE-kee)*
wild dog vekulu *(veh-KOO-loo)*
whale watamu *(wah-TAH-moo)*
wombat wamba *(WAHM-bah)*
monkey maroki *(mah-ROH-kee)*
dolphin rumpu *(ROOM-poo)*
shark zavo *(ZAH-voh)*
blobfish wubwab *(WUHB-wahb)*
fishes pazaki *(PAH-zah-kee)*
fish pezaki *(peh-ZAH-kee)*
starfish lumodoz pazaki
(loo-MOH-dohz PAH-zah-KEE)

birds taguna *(tah-GOO-nah)*
bird petra *(PEE-trah)*
parrot totu *(TOH-too)*
fox yikyik *(YEEK-yeek)*
rodent (sp) gobi *(GOH-bee)*
snake veza *(VAY-zah)*
eagle agula *(ah-GOO-lah)*
hawk haku *(HA-koo)*
bat kapa *(KAH-pah)*
deer okla *(oh-KAH-lah)*
bug banuza *(bah-NOO-zah)*
turtle totu *(TOH-too)*
otter awaati *(ah-WAH-tee)*

TIME & DISTANCE: TEMPIKO GA EEKOTOMI

**Instead of hours, weeks, or months
the passage of time on Auk Modu is measured by day, season, and turn.**

1 day *awi (AH-wee)* **= approx. 24 hours**
1 season *medidi (meh-DEE-dee)* **= approx. 2 to 2.5 months**
1 turn *nahi'medi (NAH-hee'MEH-dee)* **= approx. 1 year**

**Distance also differs from our system of measurement.
All lengths are based on a Tamariki's body size.**

1 tick *pulaga (poo=LAH-gah)* **= approx. 1 inch or a Tamariki thumb length**
1 span *pula (POO-lah)* **= approx. 3 feet or a Tamariki wing span**

SEASONS: MEDIDI

**The seasons on Auk Modu are somewhat similar to our seasons.
They are categorized by the 5 weather trends generally experienced over the course
of 1 year on the island. Each season is associated with one of the 5 realms.**

Nuna *(NOO-nah)* Twilight

the long darkness; a time for rest and renewal; associated with Tamariki

Yom *(yeeom)* Trade Winds

the windy season; a time for adventure; associated with Udara

Voltariz *(vol-tah-REEZ)* Sun Season

the hot, dry season; a time for outdoor activity; associated with Mura

Bakati *(bah-KEE-tee)* Water Blessings

the rainy season; a time for growth; associated with Awa

Galti *(gahl-TEE)* Harvest

the season of abundance; a time for celebration; associated with Yuta

NUMBERS: NUBU

The Aukipi counting system is similar to the Roman Numerical System.
Base numbers are repeated to create larger numbers.
ex: 4 (dido) = 1 (di) & 5 (do)
ex: 14 (dudido) = 10 (du) & 4 (dido)

0	vin (veen)	24	dedido (DEH-dee-doh)
1	di (dee)	25	dedo (DEH-doh)
2	didi (DEE-dee)	26	dedodi (DEH-doh-dee)
3	da (dah)	27	dedodidi (DEH-doh-dee-dee)
4	dido (DEE-doh)	28	dedoda (DEH-doh-dah)
5	do (doh)	29	dedido (DEH-dee-doh)
6	dodi (DOH-dee)	30	dadu (DAH-doo)
7	dodidi (doh-DEE-dee)	31	dadudi (dah-doo-dee)
8	doda (DOH-dah)	32	dadudidi (doo-DOH)
9	didu (DEE-doo)	33	daduda (dah-doo-DAH)
10	du (doo)	34	dadudido (dah-doo-DEE-doh)
11	dudi (doo-DEE)	35	dadudo (dah-doo-DOH)
12	dudidi (doo-DEE-dee)	36	dadudodi (dah-doo-DOH-dee)
13	duda (DOO-dah)	37	dadudodidi (dah-doo-DOH-dee-dee)
14	dudido (doo-DEE-doh)	38	dadudoda (dah-doo-DOH-dah)
15	dudo (doo-DOH)	39	dadudidu (dah-doo-DEE-doo)
16	dudodi (doo-DOH-dee)	40	dede (DEH-deh)
17	dudodidi (doo-doh-DEE-dee)	50	don (dohn)
18	dudoda (doo-DOH-dah)	100	din (deen)
19	dudidu (doo-DEE-doo)		
20	de (deh)		
21	dedi (DEH-dee)		
22	dedidi (DEH-dee-dee)		
23	deda (DEH-dah)		

MAP

REALM MOTTOS: MATI TAGIPI

Tamariki (spirit)
Do good together, live well forever.
Enlamo zuz, oragi tempiko lamo.

Udara (air)
Knowledge + Wisdom = Enlightenment
Utoko + Tago = Lumaragi

Awa (water)
Respect the sea and let the current guide you.
Kuto na'hiawa me umo kinope.

Yuta (earth)
Preserve the earth, preserve ourselves.
Ingata yuta, ingata ezuz.

Mura (fire)
Strength and courage are forged in fire.
Zu'ula ga mako vakat ai mura.

HEIROGLYPHS

Though it has been translated into English letters, Aukipi was originally composed of unique symbols and special characters.

The heiroglyphics represent specific words while the runic symbols represent each letter of the Aukipi alphabet. Both can still be found around the park today.

Symbol	Word	Symbol	Word
	RAIN		US/ALL
	FORGE		DIRECTION
	VOLCANO		INSECT
	PLANT		ANIMAL
	GROW		SEA
	LIGHT		PRESERVE
	NIGHT		WISDOM
	BIRD		KNOWLEDGE
	STRENGTH		COURAGE

RUNIC ALPHABET

English to Aukipi
translated alphabetically

a {artcl}: un (oon)

above {adj}: abawa (ah-BAH-wah)

achievement {v}: lamo'topu (LAH-moh'TOH-poo)

adventure {n}: marikawa (mah-ree-KAH-wah)

after {adv}: ogaba (oh-GAH-bah)

again {adv}: re'eto (reh'EH-toh)

air {n}: udara (oo-DAH-rah)

alcohol {n}: bizo (BEE-zoh)

all {n}: nahi (NAH-hee)

although {adv}: aga (ah-GAH)

and {conj}: ga (gah)

anger {v}: abok (ah-BAWK)

animal {n}: ezo (EH-zoh)

are {adv}: ke (keh)

arrogance {n}: okotopu (OH-koh-TOH-poo)

at {prep}: unt (oont)

award {n}: topukuto (TOH-poo-KOO-toh)

bad {n}: oko (OH-koh)

balance {v}: atana'hi (ah-tah-NAH'hee)

bat {n}: kapa (KAH-pah)

because {adv}: ka'ro (kah'ROH)

beer {n}: bizo (BEE-zoh)

before {adv}: oga (OH-gah)

begin {v}: agi (AH-gee)

beginning of time {phrase}: tempiagi (tem-pee-AH-gee)

beneath {adv}: bawa (BAH-wah)

berry {n}: kukumo (koo-KOO-moh)

best {adj}: lamia (LAH-mee-ah)

better {adj}: lami (lah-MEE-ah)

big/great {adj}: mu (moo)

bird (all) {n}: taguna (tah-GOO-nah)

bird (species) {n}: petra (PET-rah)

black {adj}: balo (BAH-loh)

blob fish {n}: wub wab (WUHB-wahb)

blue {adj}: ura (OO-rah)

body {n}: kpporu (koh-POH-roo)

boat {n}: walla (WAH-lah)

boy {n}: piwu'u (pee-WOO'oo)

brave {v}: mako (MAH-koh)

bring {v}: tupi (TOO-pee)

brother {n}: pinoo (PEE-noo)

bug {n}: banuza (bah-NOO-zah)

burger {n}: bama (BAH-mah)

bush (species) {n}: bali (BAH-lee)

butterfly {n}: kapulele (kah-poo-LAY-lay)

candy {n}: dolummi (doh-LOO-mee)

caterpillar {n}: lokolo (loh-KOH-loh)

celebration {v}: awi'zuz (ah-WEE'zooz)

challenge {v}: makoki (mah-KOH-kee)

change {n}: tokini (toh-KEE-nee)

change of heart {phrase}: ta've (TAH'veh)

children {n}: etini (eh-TEE-nee)

circle {n}: hio (HEE-oh)

Civilization

Father

civilization {n}: reroke'eto (reh-ROH-kee'EH-toh)

clan {n}: gatora (gah-TOH-rah)

climb {v}: uda've (oo-DAH'veh)

cloud {n}: hewa (HEH-wah)

coin {n}: toki (TOH-kee)

cold {n}: hul (hool)

color {n}: laru (LAH-roo)

congratulations {n}: ata'awi (AH-tah'AH-wee)

cook {v} : ummi've (oo-MEE'vay)

countless {adj}: ni'vin (NEE'veen)

courage {v}: mako (MAH-koh)

crazy {adj}: kukui (koo-KOO-ee)

current {n}: umo (OO-moh)

curse {n}: zaka (zah-KAH)

cursed {adj}: zakar (zah-KAHR)

dad {n}: pata (PAH-tah)

dance {v}: ririve (ree-REE-veh)

dark {adj}: balomu (bah-LOH-moo)

day {n}: awi (AH-wee)

death {v}: wawago (wah-WAH-goh)

deer (species) {n}: okapa (oh-KAH-pah)

destruction {n}: zakat'a (zah-KAHT'ah)

die {v}: wawago (wah-WAH-goh)

distant {adj}: kummaho (koo-MAH-hoh)

distance {adj}: eekotomi (EE-koh-TOH-mee)

dive {v}: dipi (DEE-pee)

do {v}: en (ehn)

door {n}: ki'ni (KEE'nee)

dolphin {n}: rumpu (ROOM-poo)

dream {v}: domiru (doh-MEE-roo)

drink {v/n}: ummata (oo-MAH-tah)

drop {v}: dipi (DEE-pee)

drum {n}: kaga (KAH-gah)

eagle {n}: agula (ah-GOO-lah)

earth {n}: yuta (YOO-tah)

earthquake {n}: mu'matoko (MOO'mah-TOH-koh)

eat {v}: ummiti (oo-MEE-tee)

enchanted {v}: lumari (loo-MAH-ree)

end {v}: ago (AH-goh)

end of days {phrase}: tempiago (tehm-pee-AH-go)

enjoy {v}: akili (ah-KEE-lee)

enlightenment {v}: lumaragi (loo-mah-RAH-gee)

entry {v/n}: weki'ni (weh-kee'NEE)

evil {n}: okomu (oh-KOH-moo)

exit {v/n}: weki'ut (weh-kee'OOT)

explorer {n}: arotu (ah-ROH-too)

family {n}: ta'ana (tah'AH-nah)

far {adj}: kummaho (koo-MAH-hoh)

farewell {n}: wamopua (wahm-oh-POO-ah)

father {n}: pata (PAH-tah)

favorite {n}: akilimu (ah-KEE-LEE-moo)

fear {n}: hulta (HOOL-tah)

feather {n}: yanu (YAH-noo)

feed {v}: ummiti (oo-MEE-tee)

fight {v}: ma'kove (MAH'koh-veh)

fire {n}: mura (MER-ah)

fish (all) {n}: pazaki (PAH-zah-kee)

fish (species) {n}: pezaki (peh-ZAH-kee)

floating city {n}: tana'hewa (tah-NAH'heh-wah)

flower {v}: aria (ah-REE-ah)

fly {v}: udoz (OO-dohz)

flying {v}: udoz (OO-dohz)

flying machine {n}: amara (ah-MAR-ah)

follow {v}: imitu (ee-MEE-too)

food {n}: ummi ummi (OO-mee OO-mee)

fool {n}: waki (wah-KEE)

for {conj}: va (vah)

forest {n}: yuti (YOO-tee)

forever {adv}: tempiko (tehm-PEE-koh)

forge {v}: vakat (vah-KAHT)

french fries {n}: zelu (ZEH-loo)

friend {n}: oopu (OO-poo)

frog {n}: ohu (OH-hoo)

fun {v}: ele (EH-leh)

game {n}: gama (GAH-mah)

giant squid {n}: eeki eeki (EE-kee EE-kee)

gift shop {n}: tingo'yupo (teen-GOH'OO-poh)

girl {n}: miwu'u (mee-WOO'oo)

gods {n}: taga (TAH-gah)

gold {n/adj}: ora (OH-rah)

good {adv}: lamo (LAH-moh)

goodbye {n}: wamopua (wahm-oh-POO-ah)

grandfather {n}: patamu (pah-TAH-moo)

grandmother {n}: matamu (mah-TAH-moo)

greed {adj}: okotoki (oh-koh-TOH-kee)

ground {n}: matua (mah-TOO-ah)

Growing Season {n}: Galti (GAHL-tee)

guide {n}: kinop (kee-NOHP)

guild {n}: e'ora (eh'OH-rah)

happy {adj}: ata (AH-tah)

harmony {n}: atana'hi (ah-ta-NAH'hee)

hawk {n}: haku (HA-koo)

hate {v}: ni'ta (NEE'tah)

have {v}: kinto (KEEN-toh)

he/him {n}: pi (pee)

heart {n}: ta (tah)

hello {n}: peekopua (PEE-koh-POO-ah)

help {v}: ade (AH-day)

her {n}: mi (mee)

here {n}: ki (kee)

hers {n}: mitu (MEE-too)

his {n}: pitu (PEE-too)

home {n}: tamatua (tah-mah-TOO-ah)

horned fox {n}: yik yik (YEEK yeek)

horse {n}: buzi (boo-ZEE)

hot {adj}: kal (kahl)

how {adv}: ko (koh)

hungry {v}: gaba (GAH-bah)

in {prep}: ai (ah-EE)

is/to be {adv}: ke (keh)

island {n}: modu (MOH-doo)

journey {n}: mupazu (moo-PAH-zoo)

keeper {n}: hutinka (hoo-TEEN-kah)

kingdom {n}: ke'eto (keh'EH-toh)

know {v}: utoki (oo-TOH-kee)

knowledge {n}: utoko (oo-TOH-koh)

length {adj}: eekotomi (EE-koh-TOH-mee)

less {adj}: in (een)

let {v}: me (meh)

life {n}: oragi (oh-RAH-gee)

light {v/adj}: lumo (LOO-moh)

like {v}: akili (ah-KEE-lee)

live {v}: oragi (oh-rah-GEE)

line {n}: le'emuli (leh'EH-moo-lee)

listen {v}: auroto (ah-ROH-toh)

little {adj}: ini (EE-nee)

locker {n}: lakoki (lah-KOH-kee)

long {adj}: eekotomi (EE-koh-TOH-mee)

look {v}: imi (EE-mee)

loose {v}: waku (WAH-koo)

loser {n}: wakuti (wah-KOO-tee)

lost {v}: auk (awk)

love {n}: ana (AH-nah)

magic {n}: ikoo (EE-koo)

many {adj}: mu'la (MOO'lah)

me {n}: O (oh)

mermaid {n}: kaluna (kah-LOO-nah)

monkey {n}: maroki (mah-ROH-kee)

moon {n}: nuna (NOO-nah)

mother {n}: mata (MAH-tah)

motto {n}: tagipi (tah-GEE-pee)

more {adj}: maz (mahz)

move {v}: ve (veh)

music {n}: kuluma (koo-LOO-mah)

my {n}: OO (oo)

name {n}: niva (NEE-vah)

nature {n}: yutaho (yoo-TAH-hoh)

next {adv}: wuru (WOO-roo)

nice {adj}: amata (ah-MAH-tah)

night {n}: balawi (bah-LAH-wee)

no {n}: ni (nee)

nomad {n}: aroki (ah-ROH-kee)

nothing {n}: vin (veen)

number {n}: nubu (NOO-boo)

nut {n}: luzio (LOO-zee-oh)

Observe

Shaman

observe {v}: imi (EE-mee)

ocean {n}: nahi'awa (nah-HEE'AH-wah)

of {prep}: i (ee)

old {adj} : ahi (AH-hee-oh)

old forest {n}: yuti'ahio (YOO-tee'AH-hee-oh)

on {prep}: a'i (ah'EE)

open {v}: ara (AH-rah)

or {conj}: eo (EH-oh)

otter {n}: awaati (ah-WAH-tee)

ourselves {n}: ezuz (eh-ZOOZ)

over {adj}: oba (oh-BAH)

palm tree {n}: luho (LOO-hoh)

paradise {n}: lamoragi (LAH-moh-RAH-gee)

party {v/n}: awi'zuz (ah-WEE'zooz)

parrot (toothed bird){n}: totu (TOH-too)

path {n}: pazu (PAH-zoo)

people {n}: eto (EH-toh)

phrase {n}: tagipi (tah-GEE-pee)

pizza {n}: zapi (ZAH-pee)

place {n}: tazaga (tah-ZAH-gah)

plant {v}: matu've (mah-TOO-'veh)

plants {n}: yuti (YOO-tee)

play {v}: tikitam (tee-KEE-tahm)

pleasant {adj}: amata (ah-MAH-tah)

please {adv}: nala (NAH-lah)

popular {adv}: nui (NOO-ee)

preserve {v}: ingata (een-GAH-tah)

pride {n}: wakapi (wah-KAH-pee)

purple {adj}: papura (pah_POO-rah)

rainbow {n}: larunahi (lah-roo-NAH-hee)

Rainy Season {n}: Bakiti (bah-KEE-tee)

ready {adj}: ukau (oo-KAH-oo)

realm {n}: mati (mah-TEE)

recycle {v}: retana (reh-TAH-nah)

respect {v}: kuto (KOO-toh)

rest {v}: wawat (wah-WAT)

restaraunt {n}: ummi'ke (oo-MEE-kay)

restroom {n}: wakatiki (wah-kah-TEE-kee)

ride {v}: damu (DAH-moo)

rodent {n}: gobi (GOH-bee)

run {v}: veve (VEH-veh)

sand {n}: pala (PAH-lah)

sapling {n}: yutini (yoo-TEE-nee)

save {v}: retaro (reh-TAH-roh)

sea {n}: nahi'awa (nah-HEE'AH-wah)

seaweed {n}: yutiwa (yoo-TEE-wah)

sea horse {n}: nubuzi (noo-BOO-zee)

season {n}: medidi (meh-DEE-dee)

secret {n}: migaro (mee-GAH-roh)

see {v}: imo (EE-moh)

shaman {n}: tago uto (TAH-goh OO-toh)

Shark

shark {n}: zavo (ZAH-voh)

she/her {n}: mi (mee)

shine {v}: illut (ee-LOOT)

ship {n}: awalla (ah-WAH-lah)

short {adj}: tomi (TOH-mee)

sing {v}: riri (REE-ree)

sister {n}: minoo (MEE-noo)

sky {n}: udo'oz (oo-DOH'OHZ)

slow {adj}: witoru'u (wee-toh-ROO'oo)

smile {v}: pahi (PAH-hee)

snake {n}: veza (VEH-zah)

song {n}: enri (ehn-REE)

span {n}: pula (POO-lah)

speak {v}: ipi (EE-pee)

spice (type){n}: bugroot (buh-GROOT)

spice (type){n}: tuwit (TOO-weet)

spice (type){n}: ziki (ZEE-kee)

spirit {n}: tamariki (tahm-ah-REE-kee)

star {n}: lumodoz (LOO-moh-dohz)

starfish {n}: lumodoz pazaki (loo-MOH-dohz PAH-zah-KEE)

stop {v}: wito (WEE-toh)

strength {n}: zu'ula (zoo'OO-lah)

strong {adj}: ula (OO-lah)

sun {n}: mur (mer)

Sun Season {n}: Voltariz (vol-TAH-reez)

sweet {adj}: dol (dohl)

Up

swim {v}: vewa (VEH-wah)

teacher {n}: tago uto (TAH-go OO-toh)

team {n}: gatana (gah-TAH-nah)

temple {n}: topugo (toh-POO-goh)

thank you/thanks {v}: marubu (mah-ROO-boo)

the {artcl}: a (ah)

there {asj}: obaki (oh-BAH-kee)

tick {n}: pulaga (poo-LAH-gah)

ticket {n}: titu (TEE-too)

time {n}: tempi (tehm-PEE)

to {adv}: te (teh)

to love {v}: anapi (ah-NAH-pee)

together {adv}: zuz (zooz)

tower {n} : topu'u (toh-POO'oo)

tradition {n}: narin (nah-REEN)

tree (all) {n}: golapa (goh-LAH-pah)

tree (species) {n}: banu (BAH-noo)

tree (species) {n}: totara (toh-TAH-rah)

truth {n}: hutora (hoo-TOH-rah)

turn {n}: nahi'medi (NAH-hee'MEH-dee)

turtle {n}: tuka (TOO-kah)

Twilight Season {n}: Nuna (NOO-nah)

ultimate {adj}: mu'lamia (moo-LAH'mee-ah)

under {adv}: bawa (BAH-wah)

up {adj}: uda (OO-dah)

us {n}: *ezuz* (eh-ZOOZ)

verb {n}: *hutuve* (hoo-TOO-veh)

visit {v}: *lau* (LAH-oo)

volcano {n}: *volago* (voh-LAH-goh)

wait {v}: *witu* (WEE-too)

walk {v}: *ve* (veh)

waste of space {phrase}: *wabaku* (wah-BAH-koo)

water {n}: *awa* (AH-wah)

weak {adj}: *wa'aki* (wah'AH-kee)

welcome {v}: *wahaari* (wah-HAH-ee)

well-known {adj}: *nui* (NEW-ee)

whale {n}: *watamu* (wah-TAH-moo)

what {adv}: *kino* (KEE-new)

wheel {n}: *hio* (HEE-oh)

when {adv}: *koni* (koh-NEE)

where {adv}: *kinaro* (kee-NAH-roh)

who {adv}: *kin* (keen)

why {adv}: *karo* (KAH-roh)

wild dog {n}: *vekulu* (veh-KOO-loo)

win {v}: *topu* (TOH-poo)

Windy Season {n}: *Yom* (yohm)

winner {n}: *toputi* (toh-POO-tee)

wisdom {n}: *tago* (TAH-goh)

wombat {n}: *wamba* (WAHM-bah)

word {n}: *hutu* (Hoo-too)

world {n}: *tanahio* (tah-NAH-hee-oh)

worse {adj}: *okomi* (oh-KOH-mee)

worst {adj}: *okomia* (oh-koh-MEE-ah)

yeah {adv}: *ya* (yee-ah)

yes {adv}: *ro* (roh)

you {n}: *e* (eh)

your {n}: *e'e* (eh'eh)

zero {adj}: *vin* (veen)

Notes:

thelostisland.com
info@thelostisland.com

Printed in Cedar Falls, Iowa USA by Leverage Printing.
1st edition
ISBN : 979-8-9861020-2-3